John Stonhouse

Thoughts

on the expedience of settling permanent leases with the landholders in

Bengal, Bahar, and Orissa

John Stonhouse

Thoughts
on the expedience of settling permanent leases with the landholders in Bengal, Bahar, and Orissa

ISBN/EAN: 9783337398330

Printed in Europe, USA, Canada, Australia, Japan

Cover: Foto ©Andreas Hilbeck / pixelio.de

More available books at **www.hansebooks.com**

THOUGHTS,

ON THE

EXPEDIENCE OF SETTLING

Permanent Leases

WITH THE

LANDHOLDERS

IN

BENGAL, BAHAR,

AND

ORISSA.

" It has hitherto been deemed the beft Feature in our Land Tax, that it is not fubject to Variations."

LORD AUCKLAND.

LONDON:

Printed for J. STOCKDALE, oppofite Burlington-Houfe, Piccadilly; and S. HAZARD, Bath.

PRICE ONE SHILLING and SIX-PENCE.

ADVERTISEMENT.

THIS Tract was sent to the Press many Weeks before the Author was informed that Orders were to be shortly transmitted to India, directing the present decennial Settlement to be proclaimed permanent; *an Event, which must afford unspeakable Satisfaction to Mr.* LAW, *who proposed, and to Lord* CORNWALLIS, *who recommended the Measure, and also feelingly convince the Natives of that distant Region, that this Country has a sincere Desire to promote their Welfare.*

On receiving this Information, the Author determined, notwithstanding these Sheets were almost ready for Publication, to stop further Impression, as now unnecessary. Reconsideration however induced him to give up that Design: He reflected that a Decision, which has fixed for ever the Quit-rents of the Bengal Provinces, will, doubtless, from its deep Importance, excite much Attention and Observation, and that an impartial Examination into its Expedience, will in all probability be not unacceptable at a Period, when the Resources of India and particularly the Ease and Welfare of its Inhabitants, are so much the Objects of public Curiosity and Solicitude.

LONDON, 20th September, 1792.

PREFACE.

THE Object of these Sheets is to represent, that the Establishment of a permanent Quit Rent in India is the most likely Measure to remedy the bad Effects which have been produced by the Perplexity, Oppression, and Uncertainty of past Systems of Collection.—Some short general Account of Zemindars and Ryots was thought necessary to render the Subject more comprehensible by Readers, who may have little or no Notion of these Descriptions of People, or who may not have read Sir CHARLES BOUGHTON ROUSE's Dissertation on Landed Property in Bengal. They, who are desirous of thoroughly investigating the Origin and Nature of Zemindarry Tenure and of seeing a regular and well digested Treatise on the Subject, may be amply gratified by perusing that judicious and learned Performance, which establishes the proprietary Claims of the Land-holders in India on a solid Foundation, and does infinite Credit to its Author's Ability, Candour, and Benevolence.

LONDON, 27th July, 1792.

THOUGHTS, &c.

NO Branch of the National Concerns affords a more copious and interesting Topic of Discussion than the Land Revenues of *Bengal*, *Bahar*, and *Oriffa:* They are our Refources in the East, and their judicious Management muft confequently be a ferious Object to all who wifh well to the real Interefts of their Country. On a juft and wife Syftem of Fixing and Collecting thefe Revenues, depends the rapid Profperity or inevitable Declenfion of our Oriental Empire. Few I believe there are fo callous to every Sentiment of Humanity, as to be indifferent to the Welfare of induftrious Millions, fubjected in the Revolution of Human Events to an abject Submiffion to our Power. Various and oppofite Opinions however prevail, refpecting the Means moft likely to eftablifh the Happinefs and Attachment of our Indian Subjects, on a Bafis of permanent and National Advantage, and on a Syftem of liberal Policy, worthy of the mild Domination of an enlightened and generous People.

The great Queftion concerning the Expedience or Impolicy of fixing in Perpetuity the Quit Rents demandable from the Zemindars, as the Condition of

A   their

their refpective Tenures, involves in its Determination
probable Confequences of perpetuated Evil or permanent Good to Millions of Fellow-Creatures---a Re-
flection alone fufficient to excite the humane Curiofity
of an unbiaffed Public to the important Difquifition.
Time may never again prefent to the View of Man-
kind fo extraordinary a Spectacle as that afforded us
by our proftrate Dominions in the Eaft. Diftant
Ages will learn with Aftonifhment, that an Empire
feparated from the ruling Country by many thoufand
Miles of ftormy Ocean, bleffed with proverbial Fertility, fwarming with civilized and induftrious Inhabitants, abounding in the moft beautiful and unrival'd
Manufactures, and paying an immenfe Revenue to the
Victors, was the Acquifition and Poffeffion of a Soci-
ety of Merchants.

Wifdom in our Syftem of Taxation and Government may preferve to us this invaluable Gift of For-
tune to remote Ages, and improve it to great National Advantage, may incline a numerous People to
difregard, in the Enjoyment of Security and Property,
their Subjection to a Foreign Yoke, and to contraft
the beneficent fyftematic Domination of European
Conquerors with the fanguinary uncertain Mandates
of an Afiatic Defpot. Conviction of the Expedience
on Principles of the foundeft Policy of England's
limiting her Demands of Land Tax from her Indian
Poffeffions, infpires me with an earneft Defire to imprefs my Superiors with a fimilar Perfuafion. In dif-
cuffing this interefting Subject, I am animated by the
Belief that in Pleading the Caufe of the Indian Landholder, I urge the Adoption of a Policy glorious and
advan--

advantageous for my Country. The Proprietors of Land throughout the wide extent of the Company's Dominion, expect in all the Anxiety of Sufpence, the momentous Determination, adoptive or rejective, of the Plan of Perpetuity Quit Rent, propofed by Mr. Law, and recommended in the ftrongeft Terms to the Court of Directors, by the Governor-General of Bengal. The Decifion of this grand Queftion will form an Epoch ever memorable to the Indian Land-holder; a glorious Epoch, in which a Nation in the Plenitude of Power limits its future Taxation, to confer Security and Property on its conquered Subjects; or a difgraceful Æra, in which periodical Scrutinies into the Improvements of fuccefsful Induftry are continued in a fpeculative Avidity of future Augmentations of Revenue.

To affift the Reader in comprehending this moft important Subject, I have endeavoured to methodize its Confideration by arranging it under feveral diftinct Heads. As Terms of Technical Defignation are little underftood by Perfons not converfant in Indian Revenue, a Gloffary is annexed, for the Convenience of Readers of this Defcription.

I propofe, Firft, to fpeak fummarily of Zemindars and their Right of Property in the Lands they occupy. Secondly, of Ryots and the Impracticability of the States collecting its Share of the Produce of the Lands, immediately from them, without Perplexity, Lofs, and Uncertainty. Thirdly, of the Juftice and Policy of Settling with the Zemindars, in Preference to all others, and of fixing the Quit Rents of all the Lands in India, for ever.   Of

Of ZEMINDARS
and their Rights.

THE Word Zemindar is a compound of the Perfian Words Zemeen, Land, and Dar, Poffeffor, from
the Verb Daufhten, fignifying, to poffefs, have, hold.
The etymological Meaning of the Word Zemindar is
therefore, Poffeffor of Land, and accords exactly
with the Signification attached to it, through long
Tranfmiffion by the Inhabitants of Indoftan,

The Admiffion of the Proprietary Rights of the
Zemindars to their Eftates, muft give additional
Weight to the Arguments adducible in Favour of a
Perpetuity Quit Rent. In this View I fhall make
fome general Remarks in Favour of the Validity of
their Hereditary and Proprietary Pretenfions. Though
the Word Zemindar is a Perfian compound, no Argu-
ment can be drawn therefrom, that Landholders did
not exift previous to the Introduction of that Lan-
guage into India; and that this Appellation was confidered as merely defcriptive of the Office of Superintendant of Land and Collector of Revenue. The natural Conclufion is, that the Conquerors of India,
finding the Country fhared by a Multitude of Proprietors in actual Poffeffion of their Hereditary Lands,
adopted that compound Defignation which appeared
to them moft accurately to define their Idea of the
Condition of this Clafs of their new Subjects.

The

The Maha Raja, to whom, as Sovereign, the Zemindars had paid their Revenues, was generally depofed by the Victor ; but there is Reafon to believe the principal Landholders were conciliated to Fidelity and Allegiance by Confirmation in their Lands and every Mark of Affurance and Encouragement. Defpotifm certainly *can* annihilate the Prefcription of Centuries by the Exertion of irrefiftible Authority. The Mogul Emperors however, feldom proceeded to Difpoffeffion, except in Cafes of Incapacity, Peculation, or Rebellion. Even in fuch Inftances, Policy generally induced them to prefer to the vacated Eftate, the Son or fome Relation of the oufted Proprietor.

When the Zemindar was not removed for any Crime againft the State, he received an Allowance, known by a Variety of Defignations, fuch as Malikana, Mofhaira, &c. fometimes the Malikana, &c. were allotted in Land. This is a ftrong Prefumption that the Government confidered the Poffeffion of a Zemindarry to be more than a mere Official Station, in Support of which latter Notion, the Signification of the Word Khydmut, ufed in Zemindarry Sunnuds, has been reprefented to be of great Weight. The Terms *Khydmuti Zemindarry Felaun* can however, be fairly conftrued to mean Nothing more than the Services cuftomary, and Duties attached to the Poffeffion of the Eftate: Fact, too, corroborates this Interpretation of the Word Khydmut, for the Landholders have for Centuries tranfmitted their Eftates to their Pofterity. Therefore, even if the Tranflation of the Word Khydmut into Englifh, by the Word Office, be ftrictly juft, no Strefs can be laid on it. It muft be confidered merely as a
despotic

despotic Mode of Diction, till it can be proved that the Zemindars did not, except in some very extraordinary Cases, or during the usurped Dominion of rebellious Viceroys, succeed to their Estates from Generation to Generation.

The Monarch of India considers all his Subjects as the Slaves of his Will, and Expressions of the most humiliating Abasement, but conveying by customary Association of Idea a mere formal inoperative Signification are sometimes adopted by the greatest Characters in the Empire, in their Addresses to the Throne.

A feudatory Landholder in Europe received his Estate from his Liege Lord in all the Forms of prescriptive Homage, and with Expressions of indisputable *Service*, as the Condition of his Tenure: But did the Paramount in the *later* Ages of feudal Prevalence entertain a Thought of preventing the Hereditary Transmission of the Fief. The feudal Sovereign only exacted a Khydmut, or Service, whether by personal Attendance or pecuniary Commutation. In like Manner the Forms of the Royal Sunnuds, or Grants to the Zemindars suppose them to hold immediately of the Emperor, who was not accustomed, though certainly able, to prevent the Succession of the legal Heirs.

Zemindars have been allowed by some, to be *perpetual and Hereditary Officers of Collection.*

If a Zemindarry be only an Office, and the Proprietors merely Officers of Revenue, what a singular Phenomenon does India present! What an extraordinary Deviation in Policy from every other Country is exhibited to our View! A def-

A defpotic Government appoints innumerable Officers throughout its vaft Dominions, to colleft a Land
Tax. Not fatisfied with conferring an Office of fuch
Truft and Credit on thefe Colleftors of Revenue, it
allows the Defcendants the fingular Privilege of Hereditary Succeffion to the Employment, and in Cafes
of Difpoffeffion, indulges them with a proportionable
annual Stipend for their Maintenance.

No State in the World has ever afted in this generous Manner towards Multitudes of mere official Ser-
vants. The Prefumption therefore is forcible, that
the Mogul Government did certainly confider the Poffeffion of a Zemindarry as fomething more than the
mere Charge of an Office.

The Emperor Akbar, who conquered Bengal, no-
bly limited future Demand, and fixed the Tribute to
the Imperial Court for-ever, on a moft equitable Affeffment. The Country too, when that victorious
Monarch gave this Inftance of admirable Moderation,
was celebrated throughout the Eaft for its Commerce,
Manufaftures, and Opulence. It was therefore much
more capable of bearing an annual Increafe of Taxation, than on our affuming the Reins of Government
in 1765. It was then fmarting from the recent Enor-
mitities of the Nabob Coffim Aly Khan, and obvi-
oufly required mitigated Demand and judicious Lenity, to reinvigorate and affure.

When Ultumgaws and Jaguers are granted, the
Revenue of the State, receivable from the exempted
Lands, is affigned over to the Grantee, to be collected
by

by his own Officers, who exercife in his Name, all
the ufual Financial Rights within the fpecified Limits
of his Jurifdiâion.

The Jagueendars, Ultumgadars, and Aimadars,
frequently continued the Zemindars in Poffeffion of
their Lands at an eafy Quit-Rent, and when they removed them from the Management, paid them Malikana (a Tenth of the Rent), or meafured off a Tenth
in Land for their Subfiftence. To this Day a Chout,
or fourth Part is very commonly feparated in Land or
paid in Cafh to the Zemindar, in Liquidation of his
Proprietary Claim, by the Aymadars of Bahar; a
Compenfation much exceeding the Amount of Malikana paid by the Mogul Government. It is worth
noticing, the Word Malikana is derived from the
Word Malik, which in Arabic literally fignifies Owner or Proprietor: Malikana may be therefore tranfla-
ted of or belonging to the Owner.

Surely all thefe Circumftances argue powerfully
that the Poffeffion of a Zemindarry is not merely
Official, but an Hereditary Right, derived from the
Prefcription of Centuries. Some Weight fhould, I
think, be allowed to the Opinions of thofe, who by
Experience in the Revenue, long Refidence in India,
or Official Opportunities of the beft Information, may
be fuppofed more competent than the generality to be
thoroughly acquainted with the Nature and Extent of
Zemindarry Rights.

Mr. HASTINGS fpeaks of the heritable Quality of
the Zemindarry Lands in the moft explicit Terms.

Extraâ

Extract from Mr. HASTINGS's *Minute, March*
8, 1775.

✓ " None of the Zemindars are Men of Subſtance, nor
in general is there any other Means of recovering their
Balances than by *the Sale* of their Lands, and the de-
priving them of their *Inheritance*, even when done
with the ſtricteſt Juſtice, is always attended with ſome
Degree of *Odium*, and is an Act of Severity which the
late Adminiſtration ever wiſhed to avoid."

Mr. HASTINGS,

Rev. Depart.

E X T R A C T.

Dec. 1776.

" I think it neceſſary to mention, I do not propoſe
the Appointment of Superintendant of the Bunds of
the 24 Pergunnas, but as a temporary Meaſure only,
whenever the antient Zemindars ſhall be reſtored to
✓ *their Rights*, or the Lands ſhall be let on permanent
Leaſes, ſuch an Office will certainly be unneceſſary,
as the Care of the Bunds will be left in Charge to
thoſe whoſe Intereſt it is to keep them in Order. The
24 Pergunnas are at preſent the Zemindarry of the
Company, by the *Diſpoſſeſſion* of the *legal* Proprietors,
whoſe *hard Caſe* I have long ſince recommended to the
Juſtice of the Company."

B   Mr.

Mr. F R A N C I S,

Rev. Depart.

E X T R A C T.

Dec. 1776,

" I have declared in the firſt Place, that theſe
Lands of the Provinces are not the Property of the
Eaſt India Company, but of the Zemindars and other
Claſſes of the Natives, who owe nothing to Government but a fixed Portion of the nett Produce. However, were the Fact determined by Authority, I ſhould
ſtill think it my Duty to ſubmit my Opinion to the
Company, that it is incompatible with their true Intereſt to hold ſuch a Property themſelves, that they
ought inſtantly to diveſt themſelves of it in Favour of
thoſe Natives whom I call the Proprietors, in whoſe
Hands alone it can be made Productive of a permanent Revenue; that under the direct Management of
Government, whether by Farmers or Agents the
Lands muſt fall to decay ; that if the Farming Syſtem
were not, as I deem it, an *Arbitrary Violation of Right*,
in the firſt Inſtance, it ought to be renounced on every
rational Principle of Oeconomy as *immediately ruinous to the Country*, and ultimately to that Government, which has a great and laſting Intereſt in its
Proſperity."

Extract from Mr. SHORE's *Remarks on* Mr.
LAW's *Perpetuity Plan, dated Jan.* 23, 1789.

A Compenfation is made it is true, but admitting as
I do, *the Rights of Zemindars to the Property in the
Soil*, I know not that Government has a Right to dif-
pofe of their Property in their Abfence, except in
Diftraints for Balance."

I fhall conclude the Subject of Zemindarry Claims,
by informing the Reader, that in the Year 1773, the
Roy Royan, or firft Native Officer of the Exchequer,
and the Native Regifters and Expounders of the Laws
and Cuftoms, the Naib Subahdar of Bengal, Mahom-
med Reza Khan, the Pundits or Hindoo Doctors, and
Reza Shitaub Roi Dewaun of Bahar were queftioned
by Order of Government, on the Nature of Zemindarry Property. Their Opinions recorded on the Pro-
ceedings of the Bengal Government, unanimoufly
confirm the Proprietary Rights of Zemindars, and the
heritable Quality of the Lands. The Opinion of the
Naib Subadar in Favour of the Zemindars, is in ftrict
Conformity to the Law of the Coran, which pronoun-
ces " That a Son has a Right to fucceed his Father in
" a Zemindarry, independently of any Sunnud from
" the King; nor is it in the King's Power to difpofe
" of it as he pleafes. His Right only extends to the
" receiving the fixed Revenue." The Mogul Conquerors being Muffulmen, were therefore bound by
their Religion not to Act in Contradiction to their
Holy Law, for which they had an enthufiaftic Re-
verence.

To

To them who entertain any Doubts of the Compe-
tency of thefe Natives to give a true Opinion on
the Queftions propofed to them in 1773, I beg Leave
to recommend the Perufal of Sir Charles Boughton
Roufe's Remarks on this Subject, in his Differtation,
Page 131. That Gentleman's Argumentation appears
to me unconftrained and convincing.

Of R Y O T S.

The Word RYOT is Arabic, and poffeffes a two-
fold Signification: It means a Subject in general of a
State or Country; it likewife has, by Cuftom, a more
limited Senfe, and means that Denomination of Subjects who occupy Lands held from the Proprietor, or
in Crown Demefnes, from the Government. In this
latter Signification, it is invariably underftood in the
Difcuffion of all Topics in any wife connected with the
Revenues.

A Ryot is a Tenant who *generally* cultivates the
Land he occupies, and pays a Rent as the implied
Condition of his Tenure to the Zemindar, or to the
Tahfeeldar, who is a collecting Officer appointed by
the Government to receive it.

There

There are two defcriptions of Ryots; Ryots who cultivate a particular Spot at, or very near, the Place of their own Refidence, and Ryots who cultivate Lands where they do not refide, coming themfelves or fending their Dependants to carry on the Tillage and difcharge the Rents. The latter Ryots, in Confideration of their coming from fome Diftance, generally receive more Encouragement than the former. The Rent they pay is lefs than that exaƈted from other Ryots. The Amount to be paid by Ryots is either determined by the Pottah, long Prefcription, or the particular Articles cultivated. The Rates vary in almoft every Pergunna, according to the Quality of the Land, or immemorial Ufage.

The Proportion of a Fourth of the grofs Produce, mentioned by Eaftern Writers as the Standard of Demand from the Ryots, may have been ftriƈtly adhered to in former Times; but in the prefent Day I believe it will be found, that this Rate of Colleƈtion is obferved in few, if in any Parts of Indoftan. In the Company's Dominions the Ryot is very well pleafed to receive half the Produce as his Share; and it is well known, that all over Bahar the conftituted Claim of the Ryot does not exceed the Ratio of 17¼ out of 40. Indeed when fundry Expences attendant on the Sale of his own, and Government's Share of Grain, (for he *is obliged* to take the Selling of Government's Share of Grain on himfelf) and Nuzzerati, and other Fees are deduƈted, the nett appropriable Sum realized by the Ryot is always far fhort of even this Amount.

Lands already in Tillage may be improved by en-couraging and affisting the Ryots with Money, and inducing them to cultivate Articles of a fuperior Qua-lity, for which there may be a Demand. In this Mode, a Bega (about a third of an Acre) which yielded only two Rupees, may be made to yield fix Rupees. The Ryot I confider to have a Right of Occupancy in the Land he cultivates while he pays the cuftomary or fipulated Rent, whether in Kind of Money: A Fai-lure in this Refpect entitles the Zemindar to difpoffefs him; but the Fact muft be fairly proved in the Public Cutcheny. I here fpeak only of Ryots who have cul-tivated-Lands either by expreft or tacit Confent of the Government or Zemindar for a great Number of Years. I am fatisfied the Mogul Courts of Revenue would fe-cure fuch old Tenants not in default in the Occupancy of their Lands, confidering them to have a prefcriptive Poffeffion, not defcendible to Heirs like a Zemindar-ry, but on the Death of the Tenant revertible to, and redifpofable by the Proprietor.

It may be pertinent to remark, that in all the Sun-nuds from the Mogul Government, to Ultumgawdars, Jaguecrdars, Zemindars, and Farmers of the Land Revenue, a particular Injunction to encourage and protect the Ryot is never omitted. Were a Power lodged by Government in the Zemindar, to remove at Pleafure fuch old Ryots from the Spots they have fo long tenanted, they might occafionally (though I be-lieve it would feldom occur if Government's Revenue was fixed and permanent) fuffer unjuft Expulfion from his Caprice and Refentment. Ryots who have merely cultivated from Year to Year for a few preceding

Years,

Years, without any Pottah or Agreement from the Government or Zemindar, may be regarded as Tenants at Will, and liable to be removed whenever more advantageous Offers are made for the Lands they occupy. If a Ryot whose long tenancy secures him from arbitrary Dispossession declines entering into any specific Engagements, no Difficulty or Injustice can arise, because the Inexistence of a Pottah always entitles the Zemindar to collect according to the Rate of that particular Spot for the respective Articles cultivated. Measurement is made to ascertain the Number of Begas of each Kind of Produce and the Amount Rent calculated thereon.

It must also be allowed, that there are in some Districts Ryots, who can prove the Hereditary Occupancy of their Families for some Generations, and who have been always used to pay a *certain fixed* Amount Rent. Such old Families ought undoubtedly to be allowed to plead Prescription and Custom, and to enjoy their Lands under their Zemindars at the old Rate for ever, by a Sort of Copyhold Tenure.

The Ryots who cultivate exempted Lands generally experience good Treatment. The Ryots of the Governmental Lands often fly into the Rent-free Villages with a desire to dwell and labour in them, free from the Vigilance of the Farmer; but these poor Wretches are not allowed the Liberty of choosing their Place of Residence. The Farmer's Hircarrahs soon detect them in their Seclusion, and compel them again to till in Sorrow the Fields they had relinquished.

When-

Whenever a Quit Rent in Perpetuity shall be fixed
with the Zemindar, the Ryot will *have much the Advantage*: Being unconstrained, on the least ill Treatment, he will remove to the Estate of some more con-
siderate Landholder, by whom he will be solicited and
conciliated to Industry, and be protected in the confo-
latory Enjoyment of the Reward of his Labour. Indeed such extensive Tracts are waste in the Company's Provinces, that the Ryot, when once Property
assumes a permanent Value, *will rise to a Consequence
hitherto* unknown, and the Country rapidly exhibit
in its Improvement the beneficial Effects of limited
Demand. As various Circumstances operate to raise
or depreciate the Value of Lands in different Parts of
a great Empire, it is impracticable to fix an average
Assessment for the Ryots. The Zemindars and Ryots
will settle the Rates per Bega among themselves, agreeably to the Value of the Articles of Produce where
the Lands are situated. Government should only en-
force the rigid Observance of Engagements between
the Parties. If it should interfere to tax the Ryots,
it would encroach on the appropriate indefeasible Privilege of the Proprietor. Some have urged the Facility
and Profit which would result from Government's
collecting, as Landlord, its Share of the Produce immediately from the Ryots. The following Remarks,
on the Impracticability of such a System, by a Gentleman, well known in India for his thorough Knowledge of the Revenue Collections, contain so minute
and perspicuous a Consideration of this Subject, that I
request the Reader's particular Attention to the Arguments adduced in them :

" If

" If the Ryots be declared the Proprietors of the Soil, it feems juft that they fhould be taxed in Proportion to their nett Receipts, according to the following Principle, eftablifhed by the Author of the Wealth of Nations. The Subje&s of every State ought to contribute towards the Support of Government as nearly as poffible in Proportion to their refpe&ive Abilities.

" To carry the Principle of taxing the Ryots according to their nett Receipts into Execution, the following Points muft be afcertained :

1. The Quantity of Lands poffeffed by each Ryot.

2. The Quantity of Lands, fertile or barren.

3. The Produce of the Land and the Value of it.

4. The Situation of the Lands in Refpe&t to Rivers and Markets.

5. The Allowance neceffary for Fallow Land.

6. The Expences of Cultivation.

7. The Proportion to be paid.

Thefe appear to me to be effential Obje&s of Confideration, to obtain an accurate Knowledge of the nett Proceeds of the Lands to the Ryots. Other fecondary Points muft alfo be determined, fuch as the Rate of Batta on the Rupees to be paid; by whom the

C   Pool-

Poolbundy Repairs ſhall be made; at what Period the
Tax be paid; whether any, and what Proportions ſhall
be paid for new cultivated Lands, &c. Waving, however, a Diſcuſſion of theſe, to avoid Prolixity, the
following Remarks offer themſelves on the above ſe-
ven primary Conſiderations :

1. The Quantity of Land poſſeſſed by the Ryots
cannot be known without a Meaſurement in the firſt
Inſtance, and no ſubſequent Knowledge thereof can be
kept up without conſtant local Obſervation. There
being every where waſte Lands, theſe might be en-
croached on; and the irruption of Rivers might encroach on the Land poſſeſſed on the Meaſurement.
The latter alſo, as well as the Deſertion of Ryots, might
be alledged without Foundation, were no Perſon on
the Spot on the Part of Government to detect the
Falſhood of Allegations.

This Syſtem, therefore, ſeems neceſſarily to require
that an Officer ſhould be maintained by Government,
at leaſt in every Village, to prevent Impoſitions in
Reſpect to the Quantity of Ground aſſeſſed, and even
then the Prevention of Impoſition muſt depend on the
Integrity of the Officer.

2. The Quantity of Lands can, in the firſt Inſtance,
be aſcertained only by a Perſon of local Experience;
and to render the Aſcertainments ſufficient for the
Purpoſe intended, he muſt alſo poſſeſs Integrity. The
ſame Properties are requiſite to continue a Knowledge
of the Quality of the Lands which may vary annually.

3. The

3. The Produce of the Lands of courfe may vary annually, and as the Returns to the Landlord from different Articles are exceedingly different in Amount, it will be effentially neceffary to keep up a conftant Knowledge of thefe Variations. The Price of many Articles vary annually, which would occafion further Alterations in the Tax, if proportioned to the nett Proceeds.

4. The Situation of Land, in refpeft to Rivers and Markets, muft neceffarily be confidered in the firft Inftance, and any Changes in thefe Refpefts muft likewife be attended to.

5. The Allowance neceffary for Fallow Lands could be afcertained only by local Knowledge and Experience.

6. The Expences of Cultivation involve many Confiderations : The Number of Perfons employed, the prime Coft and Wear of the Implements of Hufbandry, the Price of Cattle and Expence of Maintaining them, the Value of the Seeds, and the Intereft of the Money funk in each of thefe Expences.

7. The Proportion to be paid muft be uniform, or it could not be equal; yet, unlefs it were very moderate, the Cultivation of Rice and other unproduftive Articles muft be confiderably raifed, which by increafing the Price of the Neceffaries of Life, might be attended with bad Confequences. At prefent the produftive and unproduftive Lands are let together; a Lofs upon fome is made up upon others.

The

The above Confiderations appear fufficient to evince the impoffibility of even approximating in Practice, to the conftant equal Taxation of Ryots in Proportion to their nett Receipts.

Of the Juftice and Policy of a perpetuity Quit Rent, and fetling with the Zemindars in Preference to all others.

BEFORE I enter on this Subject, I affert it as my deliberate Opinion, that the Country, in a deplorable State, at the Company's Acceffion to the Dewanny, from the recent Enormities of the Nabob Coffim Aly Khan, has not been ameliorated in its Condition fince that Period. The various Syftems which have been fucceffively adopted by the Britifh Government in India, previous to the Commencement of the prefent decennial Settlement, have failed in different Degrees to fimplify Complication and infure Redrefs.

J Were we told, that in a certain Kingdom the Land-holders had been extruded from their Poffeffions, that Subverfion of prefcriptive Hereditary Rights had been

fancti-

fanctified by an arbitrary Pretext of concealed Refources; that rapacious Renters of the Land Tax, ar-
med with Powers efficiently defpotic, had levied il-
limitedly from the drooping Hufbandman; could we
reafonably imagine the Condition of fuch a Country
to be flourifhing, even though we fhould be further
infidioufly informed, that notwithftanding thefe dif-
trefling Circumftances, it continued to fupport the
Payment of a vaft Revenue to the State. Should we
not rather fuppofe, that many Tracts formerly inhabited
and cultivated, had become deferted and untilled ;
that Manufactures were debafed and diminifhed, and
that antient and refpectable Families, had been reduced to bewail their loft Credit and Exclufion, in the
Embarraffments of Penury, and the Mortifications of
Dependance.

How will our Concern be excited, on reflecting that
the preceding Defcription is applicable to the Bengal
Territories, injured by injudicious Speculation.

In drawing this gloomy Picture, I mean not to im-
pute to the Englifh Superintendants of Diftricts any
Difpofition to countenance Oppreffion. The Opinion formed of their Capacity for their Stations, muft
be fuppofed to depend in fome Meafure on the flourifhing State of their refpective Provinces: They
would naturally therefore, on this Account, and much
more, I am confident, from a Spirit of Benevolence
towards the Natives committed to their Care, exert
themfelves to the utmoft to promote the Profperity of
the Country, which can only be effected by an equal
Diftribution of Juftice to the Inhabitants, But it
muft

muſt be remembred, the grand Objcct of their Appointment is the compleat Realization of the Company's Revenue : A Failure in this Reſpect is dreaded
as the probable Prelude to the Diſpleaſure of Government.

To exemplify, I ſtate the following Caſe :

Oppreſſed Ryots complain ; The Collector inflicts
inſtantaneous Puniſhment on the convicted Farmer ;
The Farmer, who conſiders the Ryots as a Kind of
Property during his Leaſe, makes vehement Repre-
ſentations, and proteſts againſt the Interference ; He
foretells with inſidious Remonſtrances the certain
Ruin of his Credit with the Bankers, and prognoſti-
cates, in the Diminution of his Authority, the inevitable Loſs of the remaining Revenue ; The Ryots,
glad of an Opportunity of Vengeance, unite with the
ouſted Proprietors at the moſt critical Seaſon of the
Collections. Every Art is tried, every Intrigue prac-
tiſed which oppreſſed Ingenuity can deviſe. A ſecond
Petition for undue Support is preſented by the Farmer ; the Collector will not, however, proſtitute the
Truſt committed to him, by ſanctioning the illicit
Abwaub or extra Demand made on the Ryots, and
perſiſts in the ſtrict Enforcement of Juſtice. The Ryots immediately perceive the Chief's Determination
not to ſuffer the Contractor, like a Sovereign Deſpot,
to impoſe new Taxes at his Pleaſure. A Shower of
Accuſations for unjuſtifiable Demands ſoon overwhelms
the latter with inextricable Confuſion. His harraſſed Officers are examining Accounts, and anſwering
Charges, when they ſhould be receiving Money,
Perplex-

Perplexity and Delay enfue, the Payments flacken, and the Scene clofes with a Balance againft the Dif- trict. Government is diffatisfied, and the Deficience of this upright and fcrupulous Collector is contrafted with the compleat Realization effected by fome neigh- bouring Superintendant, whofe Diftrict has been per- haps for a Courfe of Years by far more eafily affeffed, and whofe Renters are therefore not fo ftrongly temp- ted to any flagrant Acts of Pillage and Oppreffion. The Situation is peculiar anxious and unfuitable. The collecting Officer of a large Province, furely ought not to be involved in fuch cruel, fuch perplexing Al- ternatives : In fhort, as it is obferved by Mr. SHORE, a ftrict Adminiftration of Juftice is incompatible with the compleat Realization of the Company's Revenue. Evil is fo fatally and intimately interwoven with the very Syftem itfelf, that their Coexiftence is inevitable. Palliatives have been repeatedly hied by the Benevo- lence of many judicious Collectors; but Experience demonftrates that Eradication of the inherent Princi- ple of Abufe is the only Remedy, and this can alone be effected by compleat Annihilation of the Syftem.

The decennial Settlement with the Zemindars, will, I hope, prove for ever fatal to the Farming Syftem. Punctuality of Payment, and increafe of Agriculture, will gradually evince the Superiority of long and eafy Leafes with the Proprietors themfelves, over every paft Plan of Land Taxation, Unfupported Affer- tion is refutable by fimple Contradiction : I proceed, therefore, to the Proof of what I have advanced con- cerning the real State of the Country.

Extract

Extract of a Letter from Mr. BECHER, *to the* PRESI-
DENT *at Fortwilliam, in Bengal, dated May* 24,
1769.

" It muſt give Pain to an Engliſhman to have Rea-
ſon to think, that ſince the Acceſſion of the Company
to the Duanny, the Condition of the People of this
Country has been worſe than it was before.

" In Alliverdy Cawn's Time, the Amount of the
Revenues paid into the Treaſury was much leſs than
what comes in at preſent; but then the Zemindars,
Shroffs, Merchants, &c. were rich, and would at any
Time when an Emergency required it, ſupply the Nabob
with a large Sum, which they frequently did, particularly when he was at War with the Mahrattas; the
Cuſtom then was, to ſettle a Malguzzary with the different Zemindars on moderate Terms; the Nabob abi-
ded by his Agreement; the Zemindars had a natural
Intereſt in their Diſtricts, and gave proper Encouragement to their Ryots, and when neceſſary, would wait
for their Rents, and borrow Money to pay their Malguzzary punctually. There were in all the Diſtricts
Shroffs, ready to lend Money to the Zemindars when
required, and even to the Ryots, which enabled many
to cultivate their Grounds, which otherwiſe they could
not have done. This Mode of Collection, *and a free
Trade*, which they carried on in ſuch a Manner that
the Balance moved greatly in its Favour, made this
Country *flouriſh, even under an Arbitrary Government.*

" When

" When the Englifh received the Grant of the Duanny, their firft Confideration feems to have been
their raifing as large Sums from the Country as could
be collected, to anfwer the preffing Demands from
Home, and to defray the large Expences here. The
Zemindars not being able or willing to pay the Sums
required, Aumils have been fent into moft of the Diftricts. The Aumils on their Appointment, agree with
the Minifters to pay a fixed Sum for the Diftricts they
are to go to, and the Man that has offered moft has
generally been preferred. *What a deftructive Syftem
is this for the poor Inhabitants!* The Aumils have no
Connexion or natural Intereft in the Welfare of the
Country where they make the Collections, nor have
they any Certainty of holding their Places beyond the
Year. The beft Recommendation they can have is to
pay up their Kiftbundees punctually, to which Purpofe they fail not to rack the Country where they
make the Collections, whenever they find they cannot otherwife pay their Kifts, and fecure an handfome
Sum for themfelves. Uncertain in their Office, and
without Opportunity of acquiring Money after their
Difmiffion, can it be doubted that the future Welfare
of the Country is not an Object with them, *nor is to
be expected in human Nature.* Thefe Aumils alfo have
no Check on them during the Time of their Employment, they appoint thofe that act under them, fo that
during the Time of the Year's Collection their Power
is *abfolute.* There is no fixed Huftabood, by which
they are to collect, nor any likelihood of Complaint,
till the poor Ryot is really drove to neceffity, by having
more demanded of him than he could poffibly pay.
Much thefe poor wretches will *bear,* rather *than quit*

D *their*

their Habitations to come here to complain, efpecially when it is confidered that it muft always be attended *with Lofs of Time, Rifk of obtaining Redrefs,* and a *Certainty of being very ill ufed,* fhould the Aumils influence be fufficient to prevent the poor Man obtaining Juftice,'or even accefs to thofe, able to grant it to him. On this deftructive Plan, and with a continual Demand for more Revenue, have the Collections been made ever fince the Englifh have been in Poffeffion of the Duanny. Had the proper Meafure been purfued after the Event of the Famine, probably its Effects might by this Time have been felt in a much lefs confiderable Degree, but too much Regard having been then and thereafter paid to the realizing *as confiderable a prefent Revenue* as poffible, thofe Effects have of courfe continued aggravating.

" When a very confiderable Portion, fuppofed even a third of the whole Inhabitants, had perifhed, the remaining two thirds were obliged to pay for the Lands now left without a Cultivator.

" I would alfo recommend the leaving the Lands, whenever it can poffibly be done with Security to Government, in the ·Zemindars Hands, in Preference to indifferent Izardars, although the latter may bid more for the Farms."

Extract

Extract of a Letter from Mr. Dacres, *to the* Governor-General *and* Council, *dated*
Feb. 10, 1775.

" TO grant a Remiffion in the Rents, is a Meafure,
which I have to recommend, to remedy the general
Decline of the Revenue. To remedy thefe Evils, and
to reftore the Country to a flourifhing State, there is
but one effectual Method : grant the Ryots a total Remiffion of the Taxes, which have been accumulating on
their Payments for thefe laft fifteen or twenty Years
paft ; let a Settlement be then made with the Zemindars, fixing the Rent to perpetuity, and truft to a Sale
of their Property, as a Security for their Payments."

Extract of a Letter from Mr. George Vansittart,
to the Governor-General *and* Council,
dated January 20, 1775.

" I attribute the Collections falling fhort of the
Settlement, to the Settlement having, in fome Places,
been over-rated, and in almoft every Place fixed as
high as could be afforded in a favourable Seafon, fo
that every extraordinary Accident unavoidably occafioned Deductions or Balances. This I regard as the
general Caufe throughout the Bengal Province. I ap-
prehend there is no immediate Remedy, no *poffibility
of realizing the Settlement, unlefs by reducing it to the
actual Value of the Lands.*"

Extract

Extract from Mr. FRANCIS's *Minute,* 1776.

" I think it apparent that under our Adminiſtration, the Deſire of Increaſe, invariably and inflexibly purſued, is the Ruin of the Country, and e'er long, will be found the worſt Oeconomy. Secondly, that the Mode of levying the Rents has been defeƈtive, chiefly for Want of a fixed Jumma, or Quit Rent for each Zemindarry, which has rendered the Lands of no Value from their precarious Tenure, and taken away the only Incitement to improve them. The aƈtual Employment of Farmers and Contraƈtors, while Penſions are given to the Zemindars, has been a farther Cauſe of Oppreſſion to the Ryots, and of Courſe Depopulation, by increaſing the Number of Perſons to be ſupported by the Farm, and throwing the Profits, if any, into the Hands of Strangers, chiefly reſident at the Capital, inſtead of leaving them to circulate through the Zemindars to their Tenants.

" The Country having been greatly impoveriſhed, and much leſs Land cultivated than heretofore, Taxes are of Courſe multiplied on what remains in a State of Tillage, which muſt enhance the Price of all Articles produced, as well Neceſſaries of Life, as raw Materials for Manufaƈture. There is no other Way of accounting for a Faƈt, which contradiƈts the common Principles by which the Price of Things, or the Proportion between Money and things it repreſents, is uſually determined. It is notorious, that Manufaƈtures and all other Articles are much dearer now, than when the Country abounded in Specie. In the ordinary
nary

nary Courfe of Things, the Reverfe ought to be true. In Bengal, it is not true, becaufe the heavy Exactions of Government compel the Farmer to raife the Price of his Produce, and the Manufacturer of his Labour, and their Standard regulates the Expence of every other Rank of Life.

" The Lands and their Rents being open to the Propofals of every Adventurer, and all Improvements made in them eagerly hunted after, either for the Purpofe of immediate Increafe, or to fupport fome Deficiency ; it became the Intereft, and as I *am well affured, has been the Practice of the Zemindars to depopulate their Lands, and to leffen the Value of them to Government, fince every Improvement not only fubjected them to a prefent increafed Demand, but alfo to have their Jumma or eflablifhed Rent raifed.*

" The Zemindars being thus made the Enemies of Government, have in general been removed from the Management of their Lands, but have retained an Influence over the Tenants, partly by being their Hereditary Mafters, and partly from the Expectation which the latter entertain of falling again under their Authority. This Influence they employ to embarrafs Government, by making private Collections for themfelves, raifing Complaints againft the Farmers, and putting their Ryots to flight during the Seafon of the Collections.

" The Lands being on the whole affeffed at the utmoft of their Produce in the moft favourable Seafons, (tho' in fome Places particular Perfons may have been favoured

voured with beneficial Leafes) and all the exifting
Wealth drawn out of the Pockets of the People, it
follows that Government muft depend for its Income
on the precarious Events of Seafon, Sale of Harvefls,
and good Management in the Farmers and Colleftors.
The Ryot having nothing, and never expefting to
gain any Thing, cultivates the Soil *from mere Neceffity*, and no more of it than will fupply a bare Subfiftence for him and his Family.

" I am affured that the Jummabundy, or Rent Account of every Individual Ryot, is fo confufed by ac-
cumulated Taxes on the Part of the Farmers, and
Abatements taken in the Aufful, or original Rent, by
the Ryot, that perpetual Pretences are open to each
Party, for the Fitter to cheat, and the former to op-
prefs. The Pottahs, or Leafes are fo varied and full
of Confufion, that when Complaints are made, the
ableft Muttafuddy of the Khalfa cannot tell ftriftly
who is in the right. The Neceffity of keeping up the
Revenue, generally obliges Government to fupport
the Farmer.

" In providing a Relief to the Country, I do not
fpeak of temporary Comiffion, left open to an arbitrary Increafe of Demands or future Improvements.
The Jumma, once fixed, muft be a Matter of public
Record : It muft be permanent and unalterable, and
the People muft, *if poffible*, be convinced that it is fo.
This Condition muft be fixed to the Lands themfelves,
independant of any Confideration of who may be the
immediate or future Proprietors. If there be any hid-
den Wealth ftill exifting, it will then be brought forth
                                                    and

and employed in improving the Lands, becaufe the Proprietor will be fure he is labouring for himfelf.

" The Execution of a Plan, formed on thefe Prin-ciples, will now undoubtedly be attended with Diffi-culties, but thefe, whatever they are, muft be forced and overcome. In my Opinion, the alternative is Ruin to the People firft, and then to the Government."

Extract of a Letter from THOMAS LAW, *Efq; Col-lector of Bahar, to the Board of Revenue, dated the 4th of March,* 1788.

" I received Charge of Bahar when the Aumil was in Confinement, and almoft all the Zemindars who had rented from him were either under Reftraint, or had abfconded on Account of Balances. Their Ze-mindarries were expofed for Sale if any one would purchafe, whilft thofe who relied upon Maliconnah, could not obtain any from the beggar'd Aumil. In this Situation there was nothing to take away from any one, but every Thing to beftow.

" I vifited the Purgunnah with Mounds broken, the imprifoned Aumil terrifying every petty Zemindar and Farmer with Profecutions for Arrears, and the Ryots retired into alienated Lands, as reprefented in my Letter from hence, under Date the 31ft October, 1787.

" Had I formed a Settlement with a Decreafe, al-though I might have juftly urged that the Aumil's was a nominal and not a realized one, that the average Rate per Bega, was particularly heavy from its former flourishing State, which was now reduced, and required much Expence to be restored; yet I fear that my Lenity, in that Case, to the Proprietors, would have been censured as a betraying of Government's Revenues and the Precedent as encouraging Defalcation.

" Through much Exertion, I encouraged Men of Character and Property to take the rejected Villages, and by these Means the Government obtained an Increase, and the Zemindars also a proportional one in Maliconnah, wherewith to liquidate their Debts and preserve their Estates."

Extract of a Letter from Mr. LAW, *Collector of Bahar, to the Board of Revenue, dated July* 12, 1788.

" The Expence of Hicaraahs to receive petty Sums, and their vexatious Extortions so frequently repeated, depress the poorest but most industrious Subjects.

" These, however, are not their only Sufferings: They are often deprived by Restraint, of the valuable Season for Cultivation, often prevented from reaping, always obliged to sell their Grain disadvantageously, and hence, too often punished and ruined at the End of the Year for Failures, which a little Forbearance would have averted. Even those who prove fortunate enough to clear themselves, are obliged to borrow Mo-

ney

ney at Interest, to purchase the same Grain at two Maunds per Rupee for sowing, which they sold for five Maunds."

Extract from Observations on the Farming System, by THOMAS LAW, *Esq; Collector of Bahar, dated 4th of October,* 1788.

" No Man can build, dig Wells, plant Trees, &c. or improve a Village, lest the Aumils should proportionably assess him ; if a Scarcity happen, Farmers avariciously aggravate it into a Famine, their Interest being in the Crop only.

" At the Expiration of the Period of his Lease, the Farmer's Interest prompts him to make the most to enrich himself, and render his Country less capable of an Increase, he will have aggrandised himself and kept every under Renter in Poverty.

" If a Farmer absconds, or is imprisoned, should he not have liquidated the Malikanch, or Zemindars one Tenth, Government is bound in Justice, to the numerous Landholders, to defray the Arrears from the Treasury, the former being only a Delegate. Thus in Addition to Balances, Sums must be refunded.

" The Dewanny Adawlut is at present distinct from the Nizamut, because *the strict Administration of Justice would injure Government's Revenue*, and such is the Complication of the latter System, that a separate Code is formed, and all the unceasing Exertions of a

D   separate

feparate Board with the vigilant Superintendance of
the Honourable Governor General in Council, are
requifite to keep the Machine in Motion.

" The Farmers, by over taxing the moft valuable Articles, Cotton, Sugar Cane, Opium, &c. which pay
in Coin fo much per Bega, have leffened their Culti-
·vation, and the Ryots prefer planting Rice, which is
deliverable in Kind, for if the Farmer demands more
than his Proportion, the Ryot refufes to cut it down,
and fteals enough at Night for his Subfiftence, leaving
the Remainder to rot on the Ground.

" Laftly, the Farming Syftem occafions further In-
conveniencies, Anarchy, and Defolation to Millions
of native Subjects, and Precarioufnefs of Poffeffion to
our Government.

" Within thefe *five Years of Peace and Oeconomy,*
the Burthens of Government are but little alleviated,
and the *Country fcarce perceptibly improved.* From
whence are future Armaments to be fupplied, unlefs
by the Riches'of native Subjects. Should a Drought
happen, where are the Stores of Grain for their Subfiftence. Neither will Sheds be raifed for Cattle, or
Barns built to preferve Corn, whilft Poffeffion is precarious."

Extract

Extract of a Letter from Thomas Law, *Esq; Collector of Bahar, dated November 26, 1788, to the Board of Revenue.*

" I cannot refrain from communicating the pathetic Expreſſions of the Deſcendant of a great Family.

" Our Fathers, ſaid he, for adhering to the Company's Arms, obtained Penſions and Jaghiers, and they fondly imagined that they had benefited their Poſterity by introducing a mild Adminiſtration in Lieu of Feudal Anarchy. They foreſaw not that Offices of State and Command of Troops would naturally be excluded from us by Conquerors, and that as themſelves died, the Penſions and Jaghires would be ſtrictly ſcrutinized and ſequeſtred. Under adventuring Farmers, we could not ſubmit to Extortion and Inſult, or expoſe ourſelves to Caprice for temporary Tenures. Look, Sir, into our Houſes, our Widow Mothers reduced to Penury, in vain call upon us, who have mortgaged almoſt every Valuable in their Support; our Siſters pine in Celibacy for Want of Portions and Men of Property equal to their Rank. When we look forward, future Miſery adds Poignancy to preſent Want; and the Retroſpect of paſt Splendor, aggravates all; but we have now a Hope, upon the Mocurrery Plan, that ſome may be favoured with Grants, and thoſe who have Jewels or Plate remaining from the Wrecks of their Family may purchaſe Villages, and at length, ſettle, by Degrees, to become efficient; our Gratitude increaſing to the Britiſh Government, which at once Grants us Places of Tranquillity and ſecures us from
Invaſion.

Ìnvafion, thus making the Superior Policy and Difci-
pline which fubdued us, the Source of our Happinefs.
The Look, the Manner of the Speaker, cannot be
conveyed: Much therefore is loft, yet I truft even
this faint Participation will be grateful to Senfibility
and Reafon. .

" If my Mocurrery Settlement of the Pergunnahs
Nurhut Samoy, Pelich, Behar, Malda, and Coofra,
fhould be honoured with my Superiors Approval,
though with the Referve of wanted Confirmation from
England, yet Permiffion to publifh even that Encouragement, would operate to promote Improvement
and embolden Purchafers of the Villages, where Im-
prudence or Failure may caufe a Sale. Already has
Confidence in the Syftem and in the Juftice of Adminiftration, doubled in fome Places, I am informed,
the Produce of Sugar Cane and Cotton ; thus Government will not only enfure their current Revenue, but
enrich the Country by Returns for Exports."

Extract of a Letter from WILLIAM AUGUSTUS
BROOKE, *Efq; Collector of Shawabad, and Rotas
to the Board of Revenue, dated April* 1, **1709**

" Woeful Experience of the deftructive Confequences of the Farming Syftem, excite in me the moft
ardent Wifhes for its Abolition. The very Report
has already raifed in the Minds of the Zemindars all
variety of Sufpenfe ; the marked Juftice, however Adminiftration, makes hope pre-
view with the Eye of Anticipation
the

the exhilerating Profpect : They confider it as the grand Epoch of Liberty, of Security, of Property. They look forward with Exultation to that happy Day, when arbitrary Exaction fhall be no more ; when they can meet the returning Year without Fear of vex-atious Inveftigation, or over-rated Affeffment; when Evafion and Deceit fhall be ufelefs and difgraceful; and univerfal Eafe, Profperity, and Freedom throw a Veil of Oblivion over the Sufferings of paft Uncertainty."

" I confider, that while Government's Demand is fubject to continual Variation, no Vigilance and Activity, no Experience and Probity in the Collector will be equal to a compleat Prevention of undue Affeffment.

" Periodical Equalization is fair and equitable in Theory, but Experience proves it unattainable in Practice ; that the Attempt checks the Energy of Improvement, fills every Mind with diftruftful Caution, and loofens the grand Link of permanent Intereft, by which the Subject in all Ages has been moft effectually fecured in Attachment and Allegiance.

" The prefent Syftem of collecting the Revenue, in fome Cafes, renders a ftrict and rigid Adminiftration of Juftice in the Civil Courts abfolutely impoffible. The Natives know, feel, and lament the deplorable Neceffity. Mr. LAW's Plan appears to me not merely to fimplify, but to remove the prefent Perplexities of Collection ; to be friendly to the ftric-

teft

teft Procefs of the Judicial Courts; to be a Structure erected on the Bafis of Equity, to be overthrown only by the Subverfion of our Dominion.

" Allow me, Gentlemen, to apologize for this Trefpafs on your Patience. My earneft Defire to fee fo beneficial a Meafure as a *permanent Quit Rent* carried into Execution, has induced me (though unfanctioned by official Requifition), to trouble you with this public Expreffion of my Sentiments on Mr. Law's benevolent Plan;....a Plan which with a few fubfidiary Emendations, will enfure the Relief of anxious Millions, diffufe univerfal Satisfaction through every Subordination of Landholders, and extend the Fame of our Juftice to the remoteft Kingdom of the Eaft."

Extract of a Letter from William Augustus Brooke, *Efq; Collector of Shawabad, to the Board of Revenue, dated 30th Sept.* 1789.

" I cannot, Gentlemen, conclude this Letter without expreffing my Senfe of the great Juftice of Government, in permitting thofe Zemindars, who have obtained Malikana in Land, to annex it to their Hereditary Eftates. The vexatious Uncertainty, and frequently Injuftice, confequent to the late Syftem, have, in moft Cafes, driven thefe People to apply for a tenth of their Eftates in Land. They thought it better to refign all Pretenfions to the Management of the Bulk of their Property, than to be fubject to the depredating Interference of the Aumils of Government, an Interference, which has oftentimes annihilated their proprietary

etary Rights, plunged them in inetricable Embarraffments, and rendered every Art and Evafion neceffary
to counteract over-rated Affeffment."

LORD CORNWALLIS, *in a Letter to the Court of*
Directors, dated the   of   reprefenting
the deplorable Condition of the Country, fays,

" That it is a moft defirable Object to fecure to
every Man in India, his Property, and fhield *him from*
Oppreffion, that the Company in their Wifh to ac-
complifh fo juft and honourable an End, fhould have
his moft cordial Co-operation ; but he thought in the
reduced and deplorable State of the Country, he fhould
find it an arduous Tafk indeed to carry the Intention
of the Company into Effect : That he was of Opinion
the Government fhould begin by affording to the antient Noble and Hereditary Zemindars and principal
Landholders in Bengal, the Means of *rifing above*
Poverty, and living with fome Degree of Decency."

Many of the Letters from which the preceding
Extracts have been made, have already appeared in
other Publications, chiefly however in one entitled.
" Original Minutes, by PHILIP FRANCIS, Efq;"
who, by Arguments of great Force, has with much
Ability fupported the Claims of the oppreffed Landholders, to fome ftable Settlement of their Quit Rents.
Thefe Extracts, however, compofing Part of the Chain
of Evidence here adduced, their Re-publication in
this Connexion is unavoidable; and it is prefumed the
Teftimony

Testimony of such respectable Authorities will unde-
ceive those who measure the Prosperity of the Bengal
Provinces, the Happiness of the Natives, and the
Equity of past Syftems of Collection, by the Amount
which has been received into the Company's Coffers.
We see by it what has been the Fate of our Indian
Subjects....Lamentable indeed! Can we then hefi-
tate to secure their Eafe and Comfort, by limiting Demand, and fixing it, for-ever. We
may regret the Inefficacy or Perverfion of paft
Speculation, and be liberal in the Acknowledgment
of paft Error ; but this is not fufficient: Poffibility of
fimilar Evil in future muft be prevented by fpecific
Arrangements; Thefe muft be guarded from capric-
ous Innovation, by conceded Principles of inviolable
Right. Thus a Palladium of Security and Property
would be erected for the conquered Natives of India,
which nothing but a public and infamous Violation of
National Faith could injure or overthrow. Hitherto,
an infatiable Cupidity to detect every exifting Source
of Revenue, has delivered over thefe extenfive and
populous Provinces to unrelenting, uninterefted Adventurers, who have exerted every Art to defeat the
profeffed Object of their Appointment, which was afferted to be an accurate Knowledge of the real Value
of the Lands.

Many, to procure Charge of extenfive Diftricts,
have bid more than the Lands could afford. The
Confequence is obvious; the Ryot muft groan under
the Iron Rod of Extortion.

The

The remunerative Pittance of his Labour is wrefted from him, perhaps, with Ignominy and Stripes. The wary Principle of future Profit however leaves him the bare Sufficiency of a fcanty Subfiftence. Flight is precarious; the Mermydons of the Renter environ with inceffant Vigilance the Villages of the fufpe&ed. Delufive Promifes are liberally made at the Commencement of the new Year; Pottahs are granted even with a deliberate Defign of Infra&ion: His Hopes revive with the condefcending Affurances he receives, and he cultivates once more in doubtful Expe&ation. But alas, he is doomed to a fimilar Revolution of Toil and Difappointment! Thus the private Emolument of the Farmer, and the Realization of the overrated Revenue are fecured by an atrocious Sacrifice of the laborious Peafant. Other Renters may have received from Accident or erroneous Information very eafy Contra&s. Have they, however, honeftly difclofed their a&ual Colle&ions to the Government? Far from it: They have involved their Receipts in ftudied intricacy, and enjoyed their Profits in cautious Silence, till fome envious and fcrutinizing Obferver has oufted them in their turn by a Rack-rent Offer.

The Nabob Alliverdy Khan made fome Innovations on the moderate Demands of the Court of Dhelly. Deftiny left to Coffim Aly to compleat the Ruin which preceding Viceroys had commenced. The Englifh Adminiftrations which fucceeded fhed no Ray of Amelioration over the gloomy Afpe& of Affairs. Difpoffeffion, Monopoly, and Mutability, mark with calamitous Inefficacy each Modification of the Syftem. Per-

F   plexity

plexity and Confusion have increased with each suc-
ceeding Year, and blasted all our sanguine Hopes of
Valuation through the destructive Intermediacy of
Farmers. So sensible was Mr. SHORE of the Truth
of this Observation, that in his celebrated Minute, adduced by Sir JOHN MACPHERSON, in the Year
1785, in Reply to Mr. Stuart's proposed Plan of collecting the Revenues, he asserts the actual State of the
Lands to be less known than ever, and that the Busi-
ness of the Revenue Department was such, that tho'
the Committee did indeed get through it, they could
not pretend to say it was really executed. The uniform Integrity, the Talents, and Knowledge of Mr.
SHORE, are indisputable. His Opinion, consequently,
carries with it the greatest Weight.

When we recollect the different Institutions which
have succeeded each other, when we further recall to
Mind the Gentlemen nominated to these important
Stations, Men of Ability and Experience, supported
by a liberal delegation of Authority, we cannot sup-
press an involuntary Astonishment at the deplorable
inefficacy which has attended all their measures.
Supervisors, Provincial Councils, Aumeens, and Collectors, unavailingly succeed each other through a long
Period of eighteen Years.

The unbiassed Reader, will, I think, readily acknowledge that we have had Time and Opportunity
sufficient to obtain the Objects proposed by these various Establishments. This Failure of all our Plans,

at

at firſt View, may appear rather myſterious and unaccountable ; it may however be confidently aſcribed to the following Cauſes:

Firſt Cauſe is....Diſpoſſeſſion of the Hereditary Proprietors.

Second Cauſe is....Annual Aſſeſſments, or Leaſes on very ſhort Terms.

Third Cauſe is....Continual Breach of Engagements with the Ryots, by the Farmers of Revenue.

Fourth Cauſe is....An inſatiable and inſuperable Deſire in the Farmers to make the moſt of their ſhort Leaſes uncertain of renewal.

Fifth Cauſe is....The frequent Non-payment of the Malikana, by the Farmers excepting to great Zemindars whoſe Rank and Situation made it hazardous to treat them with the ſame Injuſtice to which the ſmaller Landholders, incapable of ſtruggling for Redreſs againſt Influence, Authority, and Miſrepreſentation, were obliged to ſubmit.

Sixth Cauſe is....The Neceſſity for the Safety of the Revenue of ſupporting the Farmer with a high Hand very frequently in Acts of poſitive Injuſtice.

Seventh Cauſe is----The Collection of innumerable Abwaub or Ceſſes from the Ryots by the Farmers, over and above the legal Demands of Rent, which had been

repeat-

repeatedly pronounced illicit and publicly prohibited by Government.

Thefe are the radical Defects, to which I afcribe the Want of Succefs, which has fo peculiarly attended all our Endeavours to benefit the Country and fimplify the Collections.

Limitation of Demand, and a Leafe in perpetuity, will gradually reftore the Country, as much as it is fufceptible of Reftoration from Security and Certainty in landed Property.

The decennial Settlement undoubtedly promifes to be of great Benefit, and has given great Satisfaction to the Landholders ; but with all the Advantages which Candour can allow to be expected from it, it certainly falls far fhort, in probable Advantage, of a perpetuity Leafe.

I will venture confidently to predict, that Anxiety and Forebodings, as the prefent Leafe verges to its Clofe, will operate powerfully on the Minds of the Landholders. They will tremble at their Fate in the next Settlements. They will, in the Agitation of their Doubt, recollect that our Government formally pronounced their Right to the Malikana or tenth of the grofs Produce of their Rents ; but they will likewife recollect how ineffectually they were referred to the Farmers, and by them again to the Teekadars, or under Renters, for its Payment. No Affurances of a moderate Increafe will remove the gloomy Impreffion of renewed Scrutiny. Experience will add Vigour

to

to their Apprehenfions, and Ingenuity will be tortu-
red to devife Schemes of Concealment and Evafion.
Lands which yielded five or fix Rupees per Bega will
be cultivated with Articles of an inferior Quality,
which yield only two or three Rupees. Temporary
Lofs will be chearfully fubmitted to, in the Hope of
future Profit from a light Affeffment. During the
Influence of this general Anxiety, the Growth of National Wealth will receive a Shock, by a temporary
Ceffation from Improvement. Sufpence will freeze
the active Principle of Induftry, and the Value of
landed Property will proportionably diminifh, as few
will wifh to purchafe towards the Termination of the
Govermental Leafe.

As Inequalities of Improvement will probably appear at the Expiration of the decennial Leafe, let me
afk, What is to be done? Is the paft unjuft Practice
of countervailing the Neglect of one Man by the fuccefsful Induftry of another, to be renewed? To obvi-
ate the Neceffity of an odious Scrutiny into the actual
Value of the Lands, it is alledged, a moderate Percen-
fage may be laid in a fixed Ratio on all Rents. But if
one Man, from Want of improvable Land, pecuniary
Inability, or other Caufes, have not yet been able to
increafe his Rents, is he to be taxed equally with him,
who has enjoyed all the Means of Improvement. This
might, perhaps, be borne in a Country where the Land
Tax bears a fmall Proportion to the actual Rent; but
when the Reader is informed, that in India, the enormous Share of Nine Tenths of the Produce (after De-
duction of the Ryot's, or cultivating Tenant's Share)
is confidered as the indefeafible Right of the Government

ment, and that the ten Years Settlement is presumed to be formed with as strict Adherence as possible to these Degrees of Participation, he will immediately perceive how much a Zemindar might suffer by an additional Assessment without Increase of Means. Nothing but a new Valuation of the Lands, and all the Evils consequent to such a Measure, *at such a Time*, could surmount this Difficulty. When the ten Years Lease was made, annual Settlements had prevailed for many preceding Years. But the new Lease once formed, the Collector has nothing to do with the Valuation of private Property : His Duty is to receive the Revenue, and give no Alarm by unnecessarily indicating a Disposition to scrutinize Profits. He must therefore be supposed to be not so well prepared for the forming a second Settlement as he was for forming the first.

Permanence of Property, and Limitation of Demand, were the Settlement formed with other than the Hereditary Zemindars, would be attended with many Difficulties, and be marked by indelible Injustice. Some are strenuous Advocates for setting whole Pergunnahs with wealthy Renters, who from the Length and Security of their Leases, might find it their Interest to expend large Sums in their Improvement. Such a Measure would be a Source of inexpressible Disgust and Lamentation to Multitudes of dispossessed Proprietors. It is urged, however, that as Government would guarantee their Malikana from the public Treasury, the Zemindars would not suffer, as formerly, any Risk of its Deprivation by the Villainy of Farmers, and that having a certain transferrable Property to subsist on
which

which they never had before, fo far from being diſſa-
tisfied, they would feel the deepeſt Gratitude for the
Beneficence of Government. The Motive aſſigned
for this propoſed Excluſion of the Proprietors is, that
their Poverty prevents them from improving their
Lands, whereas the Riches of an opulent Renter would
enable, and his Intereſt would incline him to extend
Agricultural Speculations to the utmoſt.

By theſe Means it is conceived the real Wealth of
the Country would rapidly increaſe to our ſubſequent
Advantage, on Renewal of the Leaſes, without any
Violation of private Right.

This Modification of the Farming Syſtem is ſpeci-
ous, The following Objections to it, however, appear inſurmountable.

Firſt....The great Injuſtice of excluding from the
actual Poſſeſſion of their Eſtates all the Landholders of
a great Empire, on Account of the lamentable Cir-
cumſtance of their Poverty, to which our Miſmanage-
ment may have contributed, and which ſhould rather
excite our Pity and Aſſiſtance, than incur a deliberate
Act of National Violence.

Secondly....The Proprietors, fo far from being
contented with their guaranteed Malikana, would uni-
verfally lament the Loſs of Influence and Reſpect.
which would, in an eminent Degree, be attached to
the *undiſturbed* Poſſeſſion of landed Property in India.

Thirdly

Thirdly....Few, *thoroughly qualified* for the very important Charge of farming a large Extent of Country, would be found poffeffed of the Cafh requifite to effectuate, in the Degree expected, the Object propofed by this Mode of Settlement, namely, a general and fpeedy Improvement of the whole Country.

Fourthly....Thefe People being merely Renters, have no Property in the Lands. Government's Security can never be fo good on perfonal, as on real Property.

Farmers of whole Pergunnahs would be more eafily corrupted by an intriguing or invading Enemy, than numerous, and perhaps, difcordant Proprietors of fmall Eftates. This extent of Country, under the Management of one Man, on a long Leafe, would give each Individual too great an Influence, which large Offers of Money, and of permanent Leafes might tempt them to exert to our Detriment. Their Farms too, being inalienable by Sale, would remain indivifible, whereas Proprietors, who have overgrown Eftates, will, in the common Courfe of human Events, fell Portions, or the Whole, to fatisfy the Dictates of Vanity, or the Calls of Extravagance. When the great Barons in England were permitted to alienate their Lands by Henry VII, Transfer became common. Many of their enormous Eftates were diftributed for Sale amongft a Multitude of Proprietors, and ceafed to be a juft Caufe of Apprehenfion to fucceeding Princes.

Many

Many other Arguments might be advanced in Re-
futation of the afferted Advantages of farming whole
Pergunnas on long Leafes with wealthy and capable
Individuals. The few I have adduced will, I truft,
evince the Ineligibility of the Plan. The Zemindars
themfelves, then, are the proper Perfons to be accoun-
table to Government for the Land Tax of the State,
and their Property fhould be rendered valuable by immutable Conditions of Tribute and Proteftion.

The Charge on the Zemindars of total Incapacity
to manage their Eftates, is illiberal and unfounded. I
will venture to affirm, that they are in general by no
Means fo unqualified for the Truft as has been reprefented. Some of the great Landholders are certainly
fometimes Incapable of Bufinefs. This arifes from
the Ignorance and Idlenefs in which they have been
educated. *But, in Truth, Experience is no juft Cri-
terion of Decifion on this Point. When Stability of
Property, and Immutability of Demand, ftimulate the
dormant Principle of Intereft into Aftion, the Miferies
of Uncertainty will vanifh, the Love of Gain will re-
fume its Influence, and produce Prudence, Punftuality and Diligence. It is a Folly, dogmatically to
draw Conclufions concerning their probable Conduft,
under the Advantages and Incentives of a perpetual
Leafe, from their Carelefluefs or Indifcretion under
the Perplexities and Depreffions of periodical Altera-
tion.

Why the Zemindars in the Khalfa Lands fhould be
in general fuppofed incapable of managing their
Eftates, I know not. It is notorious that the Pro-
G   prietors

prietors of exempted, or Rent free Lands are attentive
to their Concerns, and informed refpecting them.
Their Eftates are generally in a more flourifhing and
improved State than thofe held under Government.
Spots where I have remarked Appearances of unufual
Care and Labour in the Cultivation, I have generally
found, on Inquiry, to belong to exempted Proprietors.   •

When the Quit Rent of the State is irreverfibly
fixed, Government is, morally fpeaking, for ever fecured in its Revenue. A real Value is inftantly' attached to the Poffeffion of Land. The Sale of a proportionate Part of an Eftate is an eafy and fimple Method of realizing a Balance of the Revenue. The
Seller is punifhed for Negleft or Extravagance in a
Manner unobjeflionable, and the Purchafer is warned
to avoid a fimilar Neceffity by the Punftuality of his
Payments. The State can have no Intereft in prohi-
biting the Sale of Land as heretofore. Facility of
Transfer augments its Value to the Proprietor, and,
by neceffary Confequence, adds to the Security of
Government. Individual Juftice may be difpenfed
without Fear of a Deficience of the Land Tax. Eftates will be fubjeft to Sale for the Liquidation of
private Debts, and the Decrees of the Civil Courts be
enforced without the Remonftrances of corrupted
Aumils. During the baleful Prevalence of the late
Syftem, the Safety of the public Revenue not infre-
quently fuperceded the Enforcement of private Right.
The Courfe of Juftice was obftrufted, or aftually fuf-
pended, and intimidating Pleas of probable Defalcation, were a Pretext to avert the Coercions of the
Civil

Civil Courts by Imprifonment or Sequeftration. How lamentable and radically defective muft that Syftem of Government be, where a fteady, uniform, impartial Diftribution of Juftice is detrimental to the Realization of the Public Revenue!

That the Zemindars fhould, in paft Times, practife every Evafion which ftimulated Craft could invent, is not furprizing. The Farmer fummons his Attendance, and fignifies the Rent at which his Eftate is affeffed: The Zemindar reprefents the exorbitancy of the Demand, and his inability to difcharge it. This Remonftrance is interpreted into contumacious Oppofition. The Terrors of delegated Authority, and the Affurances of interefted Condefcenfion, are alternately tried in irrefiftible Co-operation. He is unable longer to withhold Compliance. He figns the Caboolyat, or obligatory Deed, falls in Balance at the End of the Year, and fells his Patrimony to the Farmer in Liquidation of the Amount. This is no Exaggeration or Fiction. It has been a common Cafe. Nay, I affert as an irrefutable Fact, that more than one hundred Villages have in this Manner been furtively purchafed by a fingle Farmer, under various fictious Names.

A third of the alledged Balances were moft likely illegal, for the Farmers have a Cuftom of deducting from the Sums paid, the Amount of their illicit Exactions, and giving a Receipt for the Remainder, fo that Detection is not eafy. To exemplify....A Zemindar pays 100 Rupees his firft Kift. In vain he demands a Receipt for 100 Rupees. He can only procure one for a lefs Amount, which is entered on the public

public Books.....This, it will be said, is a direct Rob-
bery....It is fo; but it was common; and the Terror
of the Farmer was fo great, that generally fpeaking,
it was quietly fubmitted to; nay, it often happened
that a Receipt was altogether refufed. Shall we then
accufe the Landholder of Artifice and Criminality ?
The Subfiftence of his Wife, his Children, his Do-
meftics, depends, perhaps, on the fcanty Pittance he
can referve from the Fangs of Extortion. Can we then
wonder at his ftruggling for an eafy Affeffment, from
a fupercilious and relentlefs Farmer, by every Refine-
ment of Deception ? Surely not....We muft deplore
the Neceffity, and pity the Individual.

What a different Scene the Lapfe of a few Years
will probably prevent, in the enlivening Effects of
permanent Leafes ! The Zemindars, affured by the
rigid Adherence of Government to its Engagements,
will enter the Durbar of the Collector with Confidence
and Gratitude. The Collector, on his Part, unhar-
raffed by gloomy Forebodings of poffible Defalcation,
and by the Collufion of treacherous Renters, will hold
the impartial Scale of Juftice with Dignity and Firm-
nefs: He will regard the Millions committed to his
Care, with the Eye of Benevolence, and compare thefe
aufpicious Times with thofe fatal Periods, when a
deftructive Syftem rendered the Realization of the
Revenue frequently incompatible with the facred
Claims of Equity.

Can a Mind, not infenfible to the Delights of Beneficence, fail to exult in the daily Exercife of an Office which affords continual Opportunities of fupport-
ing

ing the poor and friendlefs againfl the arbitrary En-
croachmcnts of Wealth, or Power, or Influence.
Dreaded by the Oppreffor, bleffed by the oppreffed,
the Colleftor will view with undifguifed Satisfaftion,
the increafing Profperity of his Province, and employ
his Leifure in devifing Schemes of further promoting
the Happinefs of the Inhabitants. How often under
the paft Syftem did the Superintendants, embarraffed
by the Perplexities, Solicitudes, and Uncertainties of
annual Settlements, find it impoffible to attend to the
general Benefit of the Country by contriving Expe-
dients, and encouraging Improvements. Juftice however requires me to acknowledge, that many by intenfe
Application, fupported by a Determination to *diftin-
guifh* themfelves in the Exercife of their important
Offices, have benefited very confiderably the Provinces committed to their Charge, and eftablifhed among
the Natives a lafting Reputation for Equity and Benevolence. The perfonal Charafter and Efforts of the
Individual have, in thefe Inftances, qualified the baleful Operation of a counterafting Syftem.

On a Principle of limiting our future Political
Conduft in India to the Safety of our prefent Poffef-
fions, What can be more rational than to attach the
Landholders to our Interefts? Is any Plan fo likely to
effeft this Objeft as an Acknowledgment of their
Rights, as Proprietors, and a Grant of permanent
Quit Rents to render thofe Rights valuable? A few
Years without Infringement of the beftowed perpetuity
Grant, would imprefs that firm unfhaken Conviftion
of our unalterable Determination to maintain our En-
gagements, that the Value of Land would gradually

rife

rife in confequence of increafed Demand. I confefs I
cannot help indulging myfelf in the pleafing Speculation
that, in the Progrefs of Years, when a Knowledge of
the Advantages of holding Lands under our Government is difseminated throughout the various Nations
of Indoftan, Numbers, who have any Property left,
will rejoice to fecure it in our Provinces. The dif-
trafted and wretched State of many of the Countries
to the Weft, for fome Years paft, feems to afford fome
Foundation for this gratifying Suppofition. It is well
known that a Cuftom prevails in the Eaft of burying
Money, in Order to conceal it from the Violence of
defpotic Power, or to infure fome Refource againft the
Penury which often accompanies official Degradation.
How much more eligible a Mode of compaffing thefe
Ends would prefent itfelf in the Stability, Security,
and Profit, refulting from Eftates purchafed in the
Britifh Territories !

Tranquillity of Mind, Security of Property, and
Certainty of perfonal Protefion will, I am confident,
fo radicate Attachment to our Government in the
Minds of the Natives, as to form one of its ftrongeft
Supports againft Rebellion, or collufive Machinati-
ons with our Enemies, to effefit our Expulfion.

What Expefitations from the Offers of an Invader
could overbalance the Confidence infpired by *Experience* under the Britifh Adminiftration. Thoufands
and Tens of Thoufands of Proprietors and thriving
Tenants would be appalled at the very Idea of a Revolution, which fhould rifk their *prefent poffeffed* Advantages,

vantages, and throw them on the precarious Genero-
fity or uncertain Promifes of a defpotic Sultan.

It has been afferted that a Permanent Leafe would
have a Tendency to facilitate the Subverfion or Diminution of our Empire in India, by invefting the Zemindars with too much Confequence, and enabling
them progreffively to become Rich. I have already
had Occafion to Remark in Anfwer to this fallacious
Idea, that the great Zemindarries will, in all probability, be gradually fplit into a Multitude of Fractions
by Sales, Bequefts, or Donations. The Reftrictions
on the Sale of Land under the late Syftem, were calculated to promote the very Evil apprehended under a
Permanent Leafe. My own Anticipations on this
Subject, derive confiderable Probability from the recorded Sentiments of an old experienced Collector,
WILLIAM AUGUSTUS BROOKE, Efq; Refident at
Burdwan, whofe Ability, and practical Knowledge in
the Revenue, render him a valuable Servant to the
Company.

Extract of a Letter from Mr, BROOKE, *to the Board
of Revenue, dated 20th of September,* 1790.

" Senfible of the Importance of the Meafure to the
Intereft of my Employers, the general Profperity of
the Country, and the Happinefs of numerous Individuals, I have attended to the Formation of the Decennial Settlement, with an Anxiety I never before
experienced, in making an Affeffment, and with an
Affiduity, which this Anxiety has ftimulated to the
minuteft Inquiries for Information. It is a Satisfaction

tion to me, to be able confidently to affert, that I have
not over-rated any Man's Eftate throughout my whole
Diftrict. When Government's avowed Right to fo
great a Proportion as nine-tenths of the Rent, or, in
other Words, nine-tenths of the nett Receipts, after
deducting the Cultivator's Share, be confidered, it
will forcibly ftrike, that Miftakes, here and there, in
the Affeffment, can only be avoided by extreme Caution and Scrutiny....But, notwithftanding the Equity
of my Settlement, Sales will moft likely be not infre-
quent, in Order to liquidate the Company's Balances.
They will however be occafioned by the common
Contingencies of Human Life. Some will be care-
lefs and manage ill, and fome will be prodigal and idly
diffipate. Some will difcharge private Debt inftead
of the Public Revenue, and fome will lavifh immenfe
Sums in the Marriage of a Child, or the Celebration
of a religious Feftival."

Under a permanent Leafe, Charges of Embank-
ments, and Deductions for afferted Loffes by Drought,
or Inundations, will no more Occafion a Deficience in the Public Revenue. The Vigilance
and Preventive Caution of the Landholder, will
counteract, or extenuate, as much as poffible, the Effects of thefe Calamities, and of other Accidents to
which Land is liable. Wells will be dug where neceffary, and Mounds be repaired, in the moft durable
Manner, on the firft Appearance of Decay. The
Bankers will lend with Confidence, the neceffary
Sums, and Facility of Recovery, by Legal Procefs
and Sale of Affets will reduce the Rate of Intereft.
The Zemindars and Ryots have heretofore been obli-

                                                    ged

ged to pay an Intereſt from twenty-four to thirty-ſix per Cent. for Money borrowed to pay up their Kiſts or Inſtalments of Revenue: for the Farmers generally thought themſelves inſecure of Payment of any large Sums after the Crops were carried away. All the heavy Kiſts, therefore, were exacted while the Crops were ſtanding, or before they could be ſold. The Bankers knowing that Money muſt be raiſed, not only exacted the above enormous Intereſt, but oftentimes contracted for the Crop at a Price very favourable to themſelves, and not being in immediate Want of Caſh, could afford to keep the Grain in Store till an Opportunity might offer of diſpoſing of it to Advantage. It appears by this Statement of incontrovertible Fact, that the Zemindars and Ryots were doubly Victims to the Renters premature Exaction: Firſt, in being obliged to pay ſo great an Intereſt for Money borrowed; and, ſecondly, in being compelled to ſell their Crops at a Loſs, to raiſe *any Money at all.* When the Revenue is permanently fixed, the Kiſts of the Ryots may be ſafely reduced to Eight, and the Kiſts of the Zemindars to Six.

I doubt whether it may not be ſome Years before the Kiſts of the Ryots can, *with Safety,* be reduced to Six, becauſe, if the Ryot fail, he has not, like the Zemindar, a Property to make good Payment. The latter, in ſuch Caſe, could only attach perſonal Property, Implements of Agriculture, and Cattle for Tillage, which might often be very inadequate to the Amount. However, if the Kiſts of the Zemindars ſhould be fixed at Six, any Ryot, who could give Security of a creditable Banker, or other reſponſible

H   Perſon

Perfon, fhould be entitled to pay in Six Kifts alfo.. I rely on the Candour of thofe who have had practical Experience in the Collection of Indian Revenue, to juftify me for this apparent Partiality to the Convenience of the Zemindar.

If the Ryot idly fpend, and do not pay to the Zemindar, how is the Zemindar to pay to Government with Punctuality? Whatever Rates of Affeffment may be fettled between the Zemindar and Ryot, a *regular Pottah* fhould be executed, and a *Copy lodged* in the *Pergunnah Cutcherry* for Cafes of neceffary Reference. The Zemindars when acting as mere annual Renters, do not like to give Pottas, and, having given them, often revoke and annul them. Under the prefent Syftem, Inftances of this Nature will not, I think, often occur. The Poffibility, however, of fuch Oppreffion fhould be wholly prevented.

I do not mean to affert, as fome have thought proper to do, the Superiority of a defpotic Mogul Sovereignty, dependant for any good on the hazardous Contingency of individual Character, over a regulated Britifh Adminiftration. I believe however till later Periods the Mogul Government was mild and moderate in its Demand, for the Credit and Opulence which the Zemindars formerly enjoyed are notorious.

If it be faid that Moorfhud Kooly Khan, and Coffim Aly Khan plundered the Country, and difpoffeffed the Zemindars, I reply, they did wrong, and we fhould do wrong to follow their Example. Afk the Sentiments of any intelligent Native of Bengal concerning
                                                              thefe

thefe Princes? He will pronounce their Adminiftration a Syftem of Violence and Rapacity, unknown in the happier Reigns of Akbar and Aurugzebe. We fhould always bear in Mind our Situation as Britifh Conquerors, feparated from our Acquifitions by half the Circuit of the Globe, and confider what Syftem Wifdom points out as beft to eftablifh, on a folid Bafis, the Felicity of our Subjeéts, the Stability of our Power, and the Dignity of our national Charaéter. On their Principles of Juftice, Benevolence, and Policy, we may grant, adopt, rejeét, confirm, or modify, without flavifhly embarraffing ourfelves by antecedent Mogul Praétice, or Syftem, as it is generally termed, by Way of Eminence.

In Cafes where this Praétice does not interfere with Equity, and the general Good of the Country, it fhould be continued; but in Cafes where Injuftice to the Subjeét, or where Privileges of particular Defcriptions of Perfons, highly injurious to the general Interefts of the Community, are authorifed, it fhould be abandoned without Scruple, and a liberal Compenfation made to the privileged Claimants. If it be found that we have been hard Mafters, is it a Vindication to fay that fome of the Mogul Nabobs have been more fo ?

If Reformation, Mildnefs, and Equity, have been experienced by the Indians, under our Government, in the Degree alledged by fome few, How happens it that the Records under Lord CORNWALLIS's Adminiftration are loaded with Evidence of the Confufion, Injuftice, and dreadful Effeéts of paft Syftems of Colleétion ? How happens it that his Lordfhip confiders the

the Adoption of Mr. LAW's Perpetuity Village Allotment, and the Abolition of the Saier, or internal
Duties, as neceſſary Meaſures to recover the Country
from the wretched Condition to which it has been reduced. Salutary Regulations, it may be ſaid, have
at different Periods been framed for the Prevention of
Abuſe. Have they, however, been enforced on the
Farmers Revenue ? DE LOLME ſpeaking of the Æra
of Magna Charta, ſays, " From that Moment the
Engliſh would have been a free People, were there
not an immenſe Diſtance between the making of Laws
and the obſerving of them." This Remark applies to
many ineffeƌual Prohibitions of illicit Abwaub or
extra Ceſſes, and of ruinous harraſſing Chokies for
colleƌing internal Duties in the Bengal Provinces.*

Theſe internal Duties were multifarious and vexatious. They obſtruƌed Commerce, harraſſed the
Dealers, and perplexed the Colleƌors, without pro-
ducing proportionate Benefit to Government. Their
Simplification would have been very difficult and te-
dious if poſſible. Their late total Abolition by Lord
CORNWALLIS, may therefore be regarded as a Meaſure pregnant with probable beneficial Conſequence,
by facilitating the Transfer and Circulation of every
Article of internal Trade.

* The Court of Direƌors, in the 65th Paragraph of their Letter
to Bengal, dated the 10th of April, 1771, ordered the Abolition of
the Rahdarry Duties and Saier Chelunta. Deduƌions were granted
in Conſéquence. In 1786, 170 Chokies exiſted in the Diſtriƌ of
Nuddea alone. Further Deduƌions were given. Yet it is certain
that prohibited Chokies were ſtill found to exiſt in 1789.

The

The State can now impofe Excife Taxes, which deliberative Wifdom may adapt, to the Articles on which they are levied in a fuitable Manner, fo that inftead of checking, they may be found to ftimulate Induftry. The Riches of a State confift in the aggregate Riches of Individuals. When they get rich, does not Government become indirectly fo too ? The Land Rents muft remain inviolate; but may not moderate, judicious Duties on various confumable Commodities be impofed as Wealth increafes ? Certainly, Yes.....And the Government, by thefe Means, may equitably participate, when public Neceffity requires it, in the progreffive Opulence of the Nation. They who reflect on the wonderful Fertility of Bengal, the Variety of its Production, the Number of its navigable Rivers, and the Induftry of its Inhabitants, can fcarcely preferve any Moderation in their Speculations of its probable flourifhing Condition at fome future Period, even in Spite of annual Drains of remitted Revenue, *if the Revival of Commerce fhould co-operate* with certainty in landed Property to encourage Agriculture, by affording increafing Demand for furplus Produce.

Much has been faid regarding the Propriety of delaying the Meafure of permanent Quit Rents, till a more thorough Knowledge of the Affets fhould be obtained.

I beg Leave to obferve on this Queftion, that a Collector qualified for his Station, and really defirous of Succefs could not fail of acquiring in three Years of
Scrutiny

Scrutiny and Comparifon, a fufficient Knowledge of the Portion of Revenue which ought to be allotted on each Eſtate in his Province. In Anticipation of any peculiar infuperable Difficulties alledged by a Collector, preventive of fuitable Completion of the Allotment at the Time fixed, the Governor-General in Council, providently directed the Settlement of Diftricts, where fuch Difficulties might arife, to be made for *one Year only.* There may, undoubtedly, be Inequalities and Errors in the Affeffment of fome Places, but I can divine no Reafon why there ſhould be more now than at any future Period, or why, the prefent fhould not be as capable as any future Collectors, of obtaining the Information required. The Bengal Government gave long previous Notice that a ten Years Settlement was to take Place, and enjoined the Collectors to neglect no Precautions to procure by every Method, ſhort of actual Meafurement, the beft poffible Information neceffary. The Year in which the Settlement was actually formed, the Landholders were publicly told, that Application would be made to the Supreme Authority in England, to obtain its Permanence. The Importance of the Meafure was therefore thoroughly underſtood by all the Collectors, and muſt, I fhould imagine, rouze the moſt torpid Faculties to Exertion.

It may be faid, that there are fome Collectors who difapprove of perpetual Leafes. I affent to the Fact; ....But I have too high an Opinion of the Characters of thefe Gentlemen, to fuppofe for a Moment, that they would in any Degree obſtruct or retard the Execution of the Meafure when finally refolved on.
They

They would deliver their Sentiments with Freedom, and state their Reasons for considering the proposed Plan to be defective, and in so doing, they would commendably discharge their Duty to their Employers. But they would never abuse their Authority, by counteracting the Commands of Government, merely because such Commands happened not to accord with their Notions of Expedience.

To conclude, let me ask, Is Tranquillity to be disturbed? Is Confidence to be shaken? Is Evasion to be provoked? Is Improvement to be suspended? Surely the Inconveniences of some Errors in Assessment are not comparable to the probable Evils of reiterated Scrutiny and Valuation, the Result of which may be *as far as ever* from that nice Exactness of Allotment which some imagine to be so highly requisite.

I cannot bid adieu to the Reader without declaring that wholly unknown as I am to any of the Members of the Board of Controul, or to any of the Directors of the East India Company, my unfeigned Desire to see our Asiatic Subjects as happy and prosperous, as the Nature of our Relation to them will permit, has alone given Birth to this Publication. No Method appeared more likely to be impressive, than to contrast the Evils and Failure of past Systems, with the probable Benefits and Success of that proposed for Adoption; and I can with sincerity affirm, that I shall consider my time to have been most usefully employ'd if any thing I have here advanced should tend in the smallest Degree to excite, confirm, or

justify

juſtify any Intentions propitious to the Land-Holders in India.

Sovereigns of an immenſe Dominion in the Eaſt, nothing ſeems wanting to enſure the Duration of our Power, but an invariable Syſtem of Moderation, Juſtice, and public Faith. Millions of induſtrious Subjects implore Property and Protection, as the ſole Return for Tribute and Taxation : let then future Benefits drown in eternal Oblivion the Recollection of paſt Misfortunes, and let the Magnanimity of the Britiſh Character be diſplayed for the Admiration of Aſia.

SUPPLEMENT.

SOME well meaning Perfons, extremely Defirous of every Meafure, which promifes to ameliorate the Condition of the Natives living under our Government in India, may not be completely fatisfied that the great Mafs of Ryots, or (generally) cultivating Tenants, will reap fufficient Advantage, from the recently adopted Plan of perpetuity Village Allotment. I am very folicitous to eradicate any Doubts of this Nature, and therefore beg Leave to fubmit to their Confideration the following Remarks and contrafted Defcription of the paft and future expefted Situation of Ryots, In a few Particulars, I may indeed be accufed of a Repetition of what I have already urged on that Subjeft; but the Reader will more readily perceive by this concife, compaft Form of Counterview, the little Foundation there is for the above-mentioned erroneous Notion.

The Simplification of Complexity, and the future Certainty of the Revenues are undoubtedly Defiderata of great Magnitude and Attraftion, but I have no reluftance in declaring, that if Proteftion of Ryots, and Promotion of their Profperity were not to be expefted in an *eminent Degree* from Mr. LAW's Plan, it never could, by any plaufibility, allure me into an Approbation of it.

I   Under

Under the old Syſtem.	*Under the new Syſtem.*
1. The Ryots found the greateſt Difficulty in quitting Spots where they were oppreſs'd to cultivate Spots where they were not oppreſs'd.	1. They may quit on the Inſtant of bad uſage.
2. Infraction of Leaſes by the Farmers was common, when they ſaw the Crops were better than had been expected.	2 The Farmers are no more. No Demand by the hereditary Proprietor on the Ryot not warranted by his Leaſe will be allowed.
3. If a Farmer was puniſhed to redreſs a Ryot, Pleas of diminiſhed Credit, of Inability to collect, and of conſequent Defalcation unnerved the Arm of Juſtice.	3. If a Zemindar, or his contracting Agent, the Teekadar, be proved guilty of Oppreſſion, the Collector orders Puniſhment by a proportionate Fine, and Villages will be ſold to liquidate the Amount if not paid at the Time appointed. The Land Tax being fixed on each Village, Purchaſers will abound, and the Revenue of Government cannot ſuffer by a Change of Names.

4. Extra Cesses were almost universally levied by the Farmers who were uncertain of the Renewal of their Leases, and therefore made the most of their Time.

4. If any illicit Demand be exacted, the Zemindar has *no* Excuse. Being indulged in so signal a Manner himself, the slightest Oppression on his Part, merits very great Severity of Punishment. I should even propose to oblige the Delinquent to grant a Lease to the aggrieved Ryot for a Period not less than three Years, on Terms very favourable to the latter, to be adjusted by the Collector. Thus Redress would stimulate Industry in one Party, and excite Caution in the other.

5. The Zemindars, when the Farmers thought proper to put them in Possession, were generally taxed too high. Repartition of this illicit Excess on the Ryots was their only Resource.

5. The Zemindars have *now* a fixed equitable Amount to pay; *so circumstanced*, why should they be more oppressive than the Proprietors of Rent-free Lands, whose Ryots seldom complain. I have known Hundreds of Rent free Ryots, all perfectly content with a *Bilmunau-sissa Division*, or half Share of

of the Crop. In the Time of Aurungzebe, when the Zemindars were rich and powerful, there is no Reafon to believe they were oppreffive to their Tenants, who, it is faid, regarded them as their natural Lords and Protectors. Why they fhould be worfe under the Reftraints of regular Courts of Juftice, enjoying fix'd Quit Rents, and 'the utmoft perfonal Security, under an Englifh Adminiftration, it is difficult to conceive.

6. Prefcription was commonly of little Force, to protect a Ryot againft an extorting Farmer.

6. Ryot-Families will be allowed Prefcription on a Sort of Copyhold Tenure : What can be more juft ?

7, The beft intentioned Collector, I will be bold enough to fay, had not Time, under the Preffure of annual Formations of Settlement, the Charge of the Civil Court of Juftice, and the Duties of

7. Relieved from the anxious Duty of making Settlements, he can, without precipitation or Embarraffment, make the neceffary Inveftigations into alledged Grievances, and will become the Guardian

Magif-

Magiſtrate to afford that Degree of Attention which Juſtice required, to the daily and frequently intricate Complaints of Ryots.

of the Induſtrious, and the Terror of the Oppreſſive.

8. Creditable Teekadars, or under Renters of Portions of Country from a great Farmer, were frequently induced by falſe Promiſes of ſubſequent Remiſſion, to enter into Engagements for more than they could afford, in Order to deceive and decoy others of leſs Note, to accede to ſuch impoſed, exorbitant Terms. Experiencing nothing but Perfidy from the Farmers they endeavoured to indemnify themſelves by Extortion from the Ryot.

8. The Zemindar knowing that Excuſes for non Payment will not be heard by Government, and that his Eſtate depends upon his Punctuality, will be urged by Self-intereſt, one of the ſtrongeſt and moſt uniform Motives of human Action, to farm his Lands on eaſy Terms to his Teekadars. The Courts of Juſtice will *now* be able to protect the Ryots who pay to the contracting Agents, juſt as much as if they paid to the Proprietor himſelf. Incapacitation to hold any Leaſe for ten Years in that Collectorſhip, will effectually deter Teekadars from Miſconduct.

When a Fine is impoſed on a Teekadar, the Principal

Principal . being refponfi-
ble, muft pay it, and re-
cover it in his Turn
from the Teekadar, unlefs
the latter can prove he
acted by Order. This will
excite great Caution in the
Choice of contracting A-
gents of Collection.

The Owners of fmall
Eftates will, I believe, be
found with little Excepti-
on to collect immediately
from their Ryots.

One Province alone in
Bengal, it is faid, contains
20,000 fmall Landholders
called Talookdars.

9. The Ryot was never
certain under a Farmer,
what he fhould actually,
be allowed to enjoy of the
Produce of his Lands.

9. It has been afferted,
that, in the new Plan, no
determinate Rent is fettled
to preferve the Ryot from
exorbitant Taxation, tho'
we have taken all poffible
Care of his Landlord, the
Zemindar; the Ryot how-
ever is fecure. The Ze-
mindar and he know the
Value of the Begas oc-
cupied, and execute a

Leafe

Leafe founded on that
Knowledge. If the Ryot
difapproves the Terms of-
fered, he pays agreeably
to cuftomary Proportion,
a Share of the Crop.

The Rates per Bega for
many Articles vary, as
they muft in *every Country*,
in different Places. Cot-
ton Land, for Example,
may pay more in one Per-
gunna than another, from
Difference of Soil, affect-
ing the Quality, or from
Vicinity to a large trading
Town. If the ufual Pro-
portions of the Crop, or
particular known Pergun-
na Rates, are rigidly adhered to, the Ryots are content. Witnefs the few
Complaints from Ryots
in exempted Lands. The
Misfortune under the late
Syftem was, that thefe
Proportions and Rates
were continually infringed
by the Rapacity of tempo-
rary Adventurers.

10. The

10. The Kifts or In-
ftalments were payable at
Periods very unfavourable
to the Ryot.

10. Mr. LAW benevo-
lently propofed to reduce
them to fix; fuppofe to
eight. The Collector will
arrange them fo as to prevent, as much as poffible,
the Neceffity of premature
Venditure of Grain. The
ftriking off four Kifts,
which may now be fafely
done, is an Amendment
of the greateft Benefit to
the Ryots.

It appears from the above Statement, that the Ryots could never expect, under the paft Syftem, the Advantages which will naturally follow from, or which
may be fafely extended to them under the prefent Syftem. There is no Reafon, therefore, to fuppofe they
will be prejudiced by the Beftowal of fixed Quit
Rents to the Zemindars; on the contrary, that nothing
but an infamous and wholly improbable Dereliction
of Duty in the Diftribution of Juftice, can prevent
their becoming as flourifhing and happy, as their Station in Life will permit.....I may venture even to fay,
as fecure, tranquil, and comfortable, according to *their
Notions and Habits*, as a Tenant in England. What
more can be wifhed?

LONDON, October 15, 1792.

F I N I S.

GLOSSARY.

A.

Aimadar....Poffeffor of Hereditary Land, called Aima, for which no Revenue is paid to Government.

Aumil....A Native Superintendant of a Diftrict, who collects the Revenue. A Farmer of the Revenues of a Diftrict is alfo frequently called Aumil.

Aumeen....An Inveftigator, Supervifor, Regulator, Arbitrator.

B.

Bega....Mr. Holwell fays the Bengal Bega is 126¼ Feet in Length, which multiplied into itfelf, gives 16002 fquare Feet. An Acre contains 42560 fquare Feet. Therefore a Bega is to an Acre, as 367 to 1000, or as 11 to 30 the neareft.

The Bega of Bahar is larger than the Bengal Bega. A Bega meafured in one of the Diftricts of that Province produced in Length 166 Feet 8 Inches.

Bund

Bund....A Bank or Dam, to prevent the Influx or Efflux of Waters,

C.

Caboolyat....An Engagement. The Counter-part of a Pottah or Leafe.

D.

Dewaun....Native Collector General of a Province, and Judge in Civil Matters.

Dewanny....Office of a Dewaun.

Durbar....The Court of a Prince, or great Man.

H.

Huftoobood....Lit: " Is and was." Means prefent actual State of the Rents compared with former Years.

Hircarrah....Meffenger: Perfon employed to execute a Summons.

I. and J.

Izardar, properly Ijarahdar....A Perfon who farms a Diftrict or Eftate.

Jagueerdar....Poffeffor of an Eftate generally only for Life, the Imperial Revenues of which are affigned to the Grantee.

Jumma

Jumma....Amount Affeffment.

Jummabundy....Rental.

K.

Kift....Amount Revenue to be paid at a certain fix-ed Time,

Kiftbundy....Account of the monthly Inftalments of Revenue.

Khalfa....Exchequer.

M.

Malikana....An Allowance made to Zemindars, when excluded from the Management of their Eftates, being Ten per Cent on the Jumma.

Mofhaira....An Allowance alfo made to excluded Zemindars.

Malguzarry....The public Revenue : alfo the payment of it.

Muttafuddy....An Accountant. Officer of Government.

Maha Raja....The Paramount Raja, or Prince.

Maund....A Weight from 72 to 80lb.

Mokerrery....Fixed. A certain immutable Tenure.

N. Naib

N.

Naib Subahdar....Acting Viceroy Deputy of the Nabob.

Nuzzerauti Fees....Are paid to the Perfons who view and eftimate the Value of the Crops: N. B. The Expences of appraifing are fix'd at 5 Parts in 40, which deducted leave 17 ⅛, the equal Share of Government and the Ryot. But Government undertaking all appraifing Expences on Conditions of having the 5 parts added to it's Share of 17 ⅛ actually collects 22 ⅛. Therefore, nothing further ought to be paid by the Ryots. The Aumeens however always make them pay Rufoom or Fees, which is a cruel Hardfhip.

U.

Pergunna....Largeft Subdivifion of a Sircar or County. Major Rennel, to whom the Public is fo much i ndebted for his valuable Labours confiders it to anfwer in fome Degree to our Hundred. Pergunnas however are generally larger; fome of them contain 1700 Villages.

Pottah.....Leafe..

S.

Shroff....Changer, Banker,

T.

Teekadar.....An Under Renter.

U.

Ultumgadar....Poffeffor of an Ultumga or Eftate, the Financial Regalities and Revenues of which are hereditarily affigned over to the Grantee.